Chapters

Prologue

"How do I look, then?"

What could I say? Eddie was wearing a cycling helmet with a rubber swimming cap stretched over it. He had rubber gloves on up to his elbows, and his legs and chest were wrapped in silver kitchen foil. There was green make-up all over his face. His grin flashed in the dark, looking as if it was floating in mid-air.

I sighed. "You look like a twit."

Of course, this didn't bother him one bit. Not Eddie. He just went on getting ready and humming to himself. He put on his mirror sunglasses and plastic ears from the joke shop, then he asked me again.

"What about now?"

"Oh that makes all the difference," I lied. "Before you just looked like an average twit. Now you look like Dweebo, King of all Twits." Normally I would have laughed at this myself, but I wasn't much in the mood for laughing that evening. You scc, I was wearing the same things as Eddie. I looked just as stupid as he did. Worse, probably.

A thought popped into my head: just think of all the fun things I could be doing instead of this … like washing dishes or copying out a telephone directory, or something. ANYTHING sounded better than standing in this shed, feeling the draught from under the door gust against my foil wrapping. I looked out of the window. A half-moon was peering down disapprovingly from the night-time sky.

"Well, we'd better get going," I said wearily. (I said it the way people say things like, "I'm off to the dentist," or "We've got a maths test today.")

But Eddie nodded enthusiastically and nudged me in the ribs.

"Great! Let's go. Our audience is expecting us!"

This only made me more nervous. The butterflies in my stomach were doing loop-the-loops as though they were putting on a display of stunt flying.

"But what are we going to do once we get there?" I whispered urgently.

"Just play it by ear," answered Eddie calmly. "That'll make your performance fresh and spontaneous. All the best performances are fresh and spontaneous – that's what I always say."

Oh really? Well, how come I'd never heard him say it before?

We slipped out of the shed and scrambled over the wall into the field beyond. Then we crept along to another part of the wall so no one would see where we had come from. Then we clambered back over it and began to waddle up towards the house. We must have looked like a pair of seasick penguins out for a stroll. (We weren't trying to waddle – *you* try walking across a flower bed in flippers and see how you get on.) "How did I get myself into this mess?" I wondered as the back of the house came into view. "Why did I let Eddie talk me into it?" I thought as we waddled towards the vegetable patch. What had led me to this?

Well, I'll tell you – it all began a few days earlier, just before Eddie came to stay…

Chapter 1

I remember it had been a pretty normal evening. That means I was arguing with my sister, Cathy, over what to watch on TV, same as usual.

I tried an appeal to Mum, making my voice as emotional as it would go.

"But it's *Mutant Karate-Squad Kids* on the other side. It's my favourite…"

Mum is pretty tough when it comes to that sort of thing. She just ignored me. She went on pushing buttons on her calculator and looking worried. That was pretty normal as well: lately Mum seemed to spend most evenings at the dining table with a stack of bills and a calculator, trying to work out how to make ends meet.

"It's an educational programme, you know," I continued. Cathy let out a tut-tut from behind her book. (I hate it when she does that. You'd never know from the way she acted that she was my younger sister.)

At last Mum looked up. I couldn't help noticing how tired she looked.

"Tom," she said – Tom is my name, by the way, so this wasn't so unusual – "Tom, you know the rules. It's your sister's turn tonight." I could sense Cathy's victorious smile from behind her book. "Besides," said Mum, "you've got Eddie coming tomorrow."

There was no point arguing. I slumped down further on the couch. At least Eddie would liven things up round here, I thought to myself. He had been my best friend when we lived in town. When my mum and dad split up, Mum decided we should move to the country and start up the Bed and Breakfast. After that I didn't see Eddie so often, but every year he came to stay with us for a few weeks.

The opening music blared from the TV – it was Cathy's programme. My sister sat to attention.

The presenter of the show was walking along surrounded by mist. When he got close enough and the spooky music died down, he looked straight at the camera. He smiled a perfect smile and stroked his moustache thoughtfully. He looked about as trustworthy as a fox with a chicken feather poking out of its mouth.

Hello, and welcome to **Dirk Glib's World of the Unknown.** I'm Dirk Glib, here to show you that it's a strange and mysterious world out there. Tonight we're going to investigate one of the greatest mysteries of all…

"The mystery of why Dirk Glib is on TV?" I chipped in.

Cathy just shushed me. She loves this kind of thing: the abominable snowman, and UFOs, and all that stuff. Not that she believes it all. She says that scientists have to have an open mind about everything if they want to discover the truth – that's what she wants to be, a scientist.

I often wonder how Cathy and I could be so different. She's the most serious, sensible kid you've ever seen. Her way of talking, attitudes, her clothes ... even her HAIR is sensible. It's easy to forget she's just 8 years old, but then something comes along and reminds you that she's still a little kid too – like the old, battered teddy on her shelf in the middle of all her science books. Or you'll find her talking to her toy pony, but then realize that what she's saying is the Latin name for that species of pony. She's a funny mix, my sister.

"... the mystery of the Loch Ness Monster," finished the TV presenter, and as he said it, you could see the still waters of the loch behind his perfect hair-do. "Every year thousands of visitors come here in the hopes of catching a glimpse of Nessie. But the question remains ... what are these sightings of? Is the monster real, or simply a trick of the light? Perhaps even a hoax?" He smiled a smile as warm and toothy as a crocodile's.

They showed a photo that was meant to have been the monster, but it looked more like a branch to me, sticking up out of the water. The programme went on and on like this. You'd think a subject like that would be interesting, but there's a limit to how many blurred photos you can see before you get well and truly bored. I was even starting to think that I'd go and do my homework. But then Mum threw down her pen and sat back in her chair.

"Well, that's it," she said, with a sigh. "Unless something amazing happens, and SOON, we simply can't afford to keep the B&B going."

"But why?" asked Cathy. We all knew the answer, but Mum was the one who put it into words. "A B&B isn't much use if no one wants to stay in it. And no one wants to stay here, not since that wretched factory was built."

It was true: it had been weeks since anyone had taken a room. When we had first moved into this house, it had had a great view of the countryside. But that had all changed when the chemical factory was built. It sat in the distance on the horizon like a big bully in the playground, and it ruined our view. Who would want to pay good money for a view like that?

"So what are we going to do?" I asked.

Mum ran her fingers through her hair and gave us one of those smiles which people usually call "brave".

"Well, we'll just have to go back to town and I'll try to get my old job back. But don't give up just yet – the summer's not over yet, you know. We might still have a rush."

Yes, I thought gloomily, and I might build a snowman in July too.

In the background, creepy Dirk Glib droned on about the Loch Ness Monster, but we were no longer listening. Suddenly there were scarier things than prehistoric monsters to think about.

Chapter 2

I hardly gave Eddie enough time to unpack his bags before I told him the news.

We had hiked up Celts Hill on the other side of the village. With a name like that, you might think it had some ancient stones or a burial mound or something on top of it – something that might actually attract a few tourists. No such luck. Still, it was my favourite spot in the area, because you could see for miles and miles from up there. But Eddie was out of breath – the only exercise he usually got was playing video games. Once we got to the top he flopped down with a sigh. He didn't bother with the view.

"But you like it round here, don't you?" he asked, when he had recovered.

I nodded. "'Course I do. But if Mum's got to get a new job, she'll never get one round here. We'd have to go back into town." All there was in the village down the road was one tiny shop. From what I could gather, it had been run by the same person for the last three hundred years. Not much chance of a job there.

"See what you mean," said Eddie, thoughtfully. But then his face broke into a big grin. That might seem a bit rude for most people, but I knew that Eddie was not like most people. Back when we were at the same school, I was sure that he was known in the teachers' staff room as Public Enemy Number 1. He was always playing practical jokes or devising one of his money-making schemes; he was always full of ideas, even if they usually went wrong. (Like the time he had tried to collect worms to sell to fishermen, but then had forgotten about them. The worms had made a slithering break for it, right in the middle of Friday-afternoon class reading.)

That big grin was a sure sign that Eddie had one of his schemes in mind.

"What are you grinning about?" I asked.

"I was just thinking," he answered. "Did you see that programme about Loch Ness last night?"

"Yeah," I grumbled. "It was dead boring, too. Who cares if there's a real monster or not? We'll never know for sure. But what does that have to do with it?"

Eddie shook his head and put his arm round my shoulder. He had to go on tiptoes to do it. "Ah, that's why you need me around, Tom – to see the big picture... You should always try to see the big picture – that's what I say."

I shook his arm off. "What are you going on about?"

"Simple," said Eddie. "No one comes to stay here because of THAT, yes?" He jerked a thumb towards the chemical plant in the distance. I watched a plume of smoke rise from the factory's tallest chimney.

"Ye-es."

"Well, what you need is something else that they *will* come to see. What you need round here is a gimmick, isn't it? Like old Dirk whatsisname said on that programme, thousands of people go to Loch Ness to see if Nessie is real or not. Well, all those visitors have got to stay somewhere, haven't they?" Eddie crossed his arms triumphantly.

It didn't strike me as such a good plan. "That's great," I said, "except for one tiny problem. We're nowhere near Loch Ness, are we? And there wasn't a prehistoric sea monster in our village pond the last time I checked. There was a duck there, and it was a very nice duck too, but I don't think that counts as a major tourist attraction…"

"Ah, but that's where you need a little imagination, isn't it?" beamed Eddie. "People believe what they want to think is true. I mean, no one wants to think the Loch Ness monster is a just a load of bad photos of floating logs, do they? It's far more exciting to think there's a monster there. That's just human nature, that is."

"So?" Not for the first time, I didn't know what Eddie was getting at.

"Let me think about it," he said. And that's what he did all the way back down the hill. It was as if you could see the cogs turning in his brain as he thought the situation over. He was still deep in thought when we reached our back garden, and he was still deep in thought when the Number 14 bus rumbled up the lane that ran alongside the garden. There wasn't an official stop anywhere near our house, but the drivers would usually pull up if you asked them nicely. The bus stopped and out stepped Cathy.

She had been to a school fair in the next village, and she was carrying a big, silver helium balloon on a string. It had a picture of Ricky Rabbit on the side. (If you don't know who Ricky Rabbit is, count yourself lucky – it's a stupid cartoon character for little kids. It's always on TV when you want to watch something decent instead.)

"What've you got there?" I asked when she got closer.

"It's a balloon," she informed me coolly. She nodded a polite hello at Eddie.

I tried again. "OK, WHY have you got a balloon? I mean, Ricky Rabbit isn't very scientific, is he?"

Cathy looked at the balloon as though she hadn't known what was on the side of it. "I won the balloon at the fair," she said. "And for your information, helium balloons are quite interesting, from a scientific point of view."

Suddenly Eddie pushed himself upright from the garden wall. From the look on his face I could tell he had had one of his light-bulb-over-the-head brilliant ideas. "Actually there's a scientific experiment I have in mind that it would be perfect for!"

Cathy raised one eyebrow. "Really? A proper, scientific experiment?" She was never sure if Eddie was being serious or not.

"You bet it is," said Eddie. "It's a scientific test of what people will believe." He clapped his hands together, a signal for action. "OK, here's what I need. Some scissors, some marker pens and some strong tape ... oh, and any bike reflector-strips, if you have them. Nothing too heavy though."

"This isn't Blue Peter, you know," I grumbled, but I was already heading towards the house.

Eddie turned to my sister. "Cathy, have you got any of those little bulbs – you know, the ones you use for electricity experiments at school? If not, Christmas fairy lights'll do. And the smallest batteries you can find." Cathy nodded – I might have known a junior scientist like my sister would have all that stuff. She probably has all the bits you need to build a nuclear submarine in her bedroom.

We lugged everything down to the shed and Eddie shut himself in there. It took him almost two hours to get everything done. It was starting to go dark when he finally emerged from the shed. He cradled the balloon tenderly in his arms. It was now covered with tiny flashing lights and bright yellow strips.

Eddie wet one finger and held it up to test the wind.

"Perfect," he declared.

"Perfect for what?" asked Cathy. She never usually spent so long with me, but I could tell she was as curious as I was.

"Perfect for this," said Eddie, and he let go of the balloon. Because it was loaded down now, it rose slowly into the evening sky. The last rays of sunlight made the reflector strips and the silver of the balloon shimmer and flash. The bulbs twinkled and the eyes of Ricky Rabbit peered out from behind the black tape Eddie had used.

The three of us watched it soar upwards until it was just a small silver disc, twinkling with light. It looked quite nice, but so what? I didn't really get the point.

"How about that, then?" said Eddie, proudly.

I gave a puzzled shrug. "How about what?"

"Don't worry," laughed Eddie with a wink. "It'll all become clear."

The wind caught the balloon and it began to drift towards the village.

Chapter 3

The next morning things did become clear. (Well, clearer.)

"Anything in the paper, Mrs Campbell?" Eddie asked my mum innocently at breakfast. There were just the three of us there – Cathy had already eaten and gone out.

"As a matter of fact there is," said Mum and she read out the headline from the local newspaper: "Mystery object seen over Craigarth." She took another gulp of coffee. "Seems like people have nothing better to do than stare into the skies and imagine they can see spaceships." She shook her head in bewilderment – my mum prided herself on being level-headed. (She used to be a nurse. "You have to be pretty level-headed for that," she always said.)

That's my mum for you – no-nonsense. She couldn't see a scary movie on TV without snorting that it was just an actor in a rubber monster suit with a zip running up the back of it. So when people went around claiming they had actually seen a UFO for real, she had no time for such nonsense.

I stopped in mid-crunch. I couldn't believe it. Had people really mistaken our balloon for a UFO? Eddie and I swapped glances across the cornflakes. Even with his mouth full of cereal, it was clear he was grinning. I opened my mouth to say something, but a kick under the table stopped me. Eddie, of course.

After breakfast I made sure that I grabbed the newspaper so we could have a proper look at the article. This is what it said:

Several residents of the village of Craigarth telephoned local police yesterday with reports of a strange, unidentified flying object in the skies early yesterday evening. One caller described the object as "round and silver, with lights that flashed on and off." Another said "I've never seen anything like it before." One or two callers even claimed that the object had flown so low that they could see a strange face peering out of a window: "I don't know what it was, but it didn't look human," revealed one caller, who did not give her name. "It looked friendly, but you never know, do you?"

Local police said that the object was probably a small aeroplane or helicopter.

"But what's all this about seeing a face?" I asked.

"That must have been what you could still see of Ricky Rabbit on the side of the balloon! Best thing that creepy rabbit ever did, if you ask me."

I crossed my arms and once again marvelled at how weird Eddie could be.

"OK, you proved your point," I said. "But so what?"

Eddie tossed the newspaper to one side and flopped down on the couch. "Now we just sit back and wait." He clicked the TV on with the remote control. I couldn't stop thinking about that newspaper article, but I knew that I would have to question Eddie in a more private place than this, without any chance of being overheard.

It wasn't long before the phone rang in the hall. Mum answered it, and a few minutes later she bustled into the room. She was dragging the vacuum cleaner behind her.

"Right, look sharp you two," she said brightly. "We've got guests staying today. A group booking – five of them – and they arrive this afternoon. So we don't want them being put off when they see two zombies in the living room, now, do we?"

"Ha, ha, very funny," I replied without moving.

"Or maybe they'll just think you're some kind of trendy new furniture and sit on you." She poked me in the ribs with the vacuum handle. "Up you get."

I hauled myself up. "I can take a hint," I said. In fact, I was glad to see the mood Mum was in – this was the most cheerful I'd seen her in weeks. "C'mon, Eddie. Let's go down to the village."

Chapter 4

Things had changed overnight there. It used to be what people call a "sleepy, little village". Well, the sleepy village was wide awake now. There was a buzz of excitement in the air.

All along the High Street people stood in pairs or small groups, deep in serious conversation. Neighbours spoke over garden fences. People walking dogs stood talking at street corners, while their dogs tried in vain to pull them towards lamp-posts. And everyone was talking about the same thing. As we walked past them, we caught snippets of conversations held in anxious whispers. Things like:

"Why here? Why us?"

"Who knows if they're friendly?"

"You saw that film, *Gooby, the Kid from Space*, didn't you? That was a friendly little alien…"

"Yeah, but I saw *Killer Invasion from Beyond,* too. Not much friendly about trying to eat people."

"Well, I kept watch all night with a pitch-fork in my hands."

"Yeah, I kept a cricket bat next to the bed."

I gripped Eddie's arm and hurried him down the road until we were out of earshot. Once we reached the bench at the duck pond, we could talk safely.

"Listen to them," I hissed. "They all really think it was a UFO."

"Yeah!" beamed Eddie. "Great, eh?"

I shook my head – I hadn't imagined people would take it so seriously – but Eddie pressed on. "Besides," he said, "didn't you see the looks on their faces? They love it!"

I had to admit, it was true – the villagers seemed anxious, but there was also a kind of excited glow on their faces. (It reminded me a bit of when my Grandad used to talk about growing up in the war: "Air raids, food rationing, the threat of a bomb falling on your bonce…" he'd say. Then he'd smile and add, "Best days of my life.")

"This is just the ticket," continued Eddie. "Like I said, all you needed was a gimmick. Now you've got one, people'll be queuing up to stay at the Bed and Breakfast."

It was true: we had only just seen the local paper, and already the B&B was almost full for the night. It couldn't be a coincidence. Maybe this really was an answer to our problems. So why did I have that knot in my stomach? Either I had eaten too much at breakfast, or I was getting a bad feeling about all of this.

Just then I spotted Cathy. She was riding her bike as fast as she could, standing up on the pedals to get extra speed, and she was coming right this way. Her brakes squealed as she pulled up in front of us. I saw that she had a copy of the newspaper tucked under her arm.

My little sister narrowed her eyes and stared straight at me. (I hate it when she does that. There's something about that look of hers that makes me feel like a naughty little kid.)

"I think you two have got some explaining to do," Cathy said, sounding like a stern headteacher.

It wasn't an easy job convincing Cathy. At first she just crossed her arms and said, "It's lying! You've got to tell the truth before you get yourselves into lots of trouble."

"What do you mean, 'yourselves'?" I asked. "You helped too!"

"Yes, but I didn't know what you were up to." She sounded pretty determined, and I thought she was going to cycle off there and then and tell Mum.

But then Eddie went to work. He can be very persuasive when he tries, and right now he was trying his hardest. "You know, in a way, it's not really lying, is it? I mean, all we did was decorate a balloon and let it go. It's not our fault if people got the wrong end of the stick, is it?"

"Well ..."

"And no one's asking you actually to tell any lies. All you have to do is keep quiet, for just a little longer."

"I'm not sure ..."

What finally won her over was the news about the five guests coming to the B&B. I could see it was a tough choice for her: on the one hand, she wanted to tell the truth about the whole thing. (As a young scientist, truth and accuracy were very important to her.) On the other hand, she didn't want to ruin our family's chances of staying in the B&B. I knew Cathy was just as worried about our future as I was. None of us wanted to leave the village.

At last she let out a heavy sigh. "OK, I'll keep quiet about it all … but just for a while."

Chapter 5

The guests for the B&B arrived later that afternoon. They came in an ancient van, which coughed and spluttered its way up the road. It pulled up outside the house and the five people got out, two women and three men. They stretched and yawned and blinked in the sunshine. They all had T-shirts on with pictures of flying saucers and aliens and things like that. Here's what the slogans on the five T-shirts said:

They all had either a camera or a pair of binoculars around their necks, and I saw the barrels of telescopes poking out from a couple of bags. One of the group, a big man with a bushy beard, strolled up to me and Eddie.

"Just drove 150 miles to get here," he smiled proudly. "We're booked in for the night."

"What's the name?" I asked.

"Stuffo."

Now, I don't know about you, but that strikes me as a bit rude when you've only just met someone. Why was this man saying "stuffo" to me, I wondered, and what did it mean? What I said was: "Pardon?"

"STUFFO. That's the name we're booked under, and that's who we are. The Society for Tracking Unidentified Friendly Flying Objects."

"Why 'friendly'?" asked Eddie.

The man rolled his eyes. "Are you crazy, lad? Who wants to tangle with an *unfriendly* flying object? Don't want to get burnt to a frazzle by alien blasters, do you?"

"Not especially," agreed Eddie.

"Well then," said the man, as if that explained everything. The others nodded in agreement behind him. Several woolly hats bobbled.

"So … er … what does your society do?" I asked.

"Have you ever heard of 'twitchers'?" asked one of the women, thumbing her glasses up her nose. She looked quickly over each shoulder as if she was checking that no one could hear her. (No one could, unless you count the pigeons, and the pigeons aren't too bright round our way.)

A vacant look settled on Eddie's face, but I nodded. I used to like bird-watching, so I knew all about twitchers. They were the bird-watchers who were so dedicated that they would drop anything and zoom off to a remote part of the country, if a rare bird was sighted there.

The woman in glasses stared at us. I got the feeling that she was trying to decide if we could be trusted. "Well," she said, "we're just like them, only we look for something bigger than birds. We look for UFOs."

"You mean you heard about the sighting here already?" gasped Eddie. I could tell he was impressed. After all, the article had only appeared in our local paper, as far as we knew.

"That is affirmative," said a skinny man. "We're linked on-line so that we can maintain a constant real-time interface and download all relevant data." He said some other stuff which made even less sense to me. His Adam's apple jiggled excitedly as he spoke.

"Eh?"

Bushy Beard translated for us. (Of course, he wasn't really called that. I found out their real names later, but I'm not going to use them here, just in case any of the members of STUFFO live near you.) "What he means," said Bushy Beard, "is we all stay in touch by computer, so we can find out what's going on. The five of us, we're just the first – advance troops, if you like – but there'll be plenty more along later. You can bet on it."

Eddie gave me a nudge in the ribs, and I knew what he meant by it. He had been right – just because of one silly trick with a balloon, here were people staying at the B&B again. And more to come!

"So … did either of you two see anything unusual last night?" asked the other woman. She peered at us from beneath a fringe of frizzy hair and her eyes glittered with curiosity. All five of them leaned forward eagerly to hear our answers. The man with an anorak and a bowl-haircut held his pen ready over a notebook. I gulped and tried to think.

Luckily Eddie jumped in. "Funny you should mention it," he answered, "but we did see something a bit odd, didn't we Tom?" I just nodded dumbly. "Some kind of circular object with lights on it."

The five nodded at each other.

"Type C Sighting, by the sounds of it," declared the woman with frizzy hair. She sounded breathless with excitement. The others murmured agreement.

"What's a Type C sighting?" asked Eddie.

"Clear sighting of an unidentified flying object," declared Bushy Beard, sounding as if he was reading a definition out of a dictionary. He seemed to be the leader of this odd group of people.

"And a Type B sighting?"

The man with the bowl-haircut and the notebook said something, but he spoke so softly and held his head so low that I couldn't make it out.

"Pardon?"

The man with the bowl-cut went scarlet with embarrassment. He whispered his comment again to the woman with glasses. She nodded agreement and said, "Yes, that's a sighting, from a distance, of your actual aliens on the

25

ground. You know, collecting samples of plant-life, and so on..."

"And Type A?" asked Eddie. He was enjoying himself.

All five of them gave a little shiver of excitement at the very mention of a Type A sighting. "That's the big one," the woman with frizzy hair said in an awed tone. "The one we're all waiting for – the first meeting."

What are we getting ourselves into? I thought to myself nervously. But all I said was: "You'd better follow me. I'll show you to your rooms."

Chapter 6

The next morning I opened my eyes and saw Eddie standing over me.

"Wakey, wakey! Time to get up, you slob!" he said. (That's "Good morning," in Eddie-speak.) It wasn't the most pleasant way to wake up, to be honest.

I yawned and rubbed my eyes. It had been a late night. Eddie and I had stayed up and watched the five members of STUFFO.

As soon as it had gone dark, the five had put on their anoraks and woolly hats, and set up their equipment in the back garden. Then they had all sat down in folding lawn-chairs, and just waited. Every so often they passed around a flask of hot soup. Eddie and I had watched them for three hours. In that time, just three things had happened. First, all five had grown excited when they spotted a light in the sky – it turned out to be a small aeroplane. Second, they had heard an odd rustling in the bushes in the garden – it had turned out to be a hedgehog. Third, the skinny man had jumped up and shouted "YAH!" at the top of his voice. It turned out he had spilt tomato and lentil soup in his lap.

All in all, not much activity for three hours. Still, I told myself, you can't pick and choose who you want to stay at the B&B. The members of STUFFO paid their money, same as anyone else.

I threw on my clothes and we charged downstairs. The five of them were already in the breakfast room. As we went by on our way to the kitchen, I heard them discussing some UFO sighting that had occurred in America. The woman with frizzy hair was eagerly telling the others that, under hypnosis, some man had remembered being beamed on to an alien ship.

The aliens had asked him dozens of questions, she said, before beaming him back down to his pick-up truck in the desert.

The woman in glasses nodded and said that the American government had hushed the whole thing up. As far as I could tell, she thought all governments knew that UFOs existed, but they all kept them a secret from the people. I wasn't sure why.

I shook my head in amazement. Didn't these people talk about anything else?

I could hear the clatter of pans and the sizzle of bacon. We followed our noses to the kitchen, where Mum was getting breakfast ready.

Eddie took up position at the kitchen table and poured himself a small mountain of cereal. Before I could join him, Mum said to me, "Hold on – you can make yourself useful. Take these breakfasts in, will you?"

So I carried the two plates into the guests' breakfast room and set them in front of Bushy Beard and the woman with the glasses.

"So how did your observation go last night?" I asked.

Bushy Beard stroked his beard, an action that did not completely rid it of toast crumbs.

"Not bad, lad, not bad," he said cautiously.

"Did you see anything?"

The man with the bowl-haircut pulled out his notebook. (He seemed to carry it at all times.) His face became the colour of a radish as he whispered to the skinny man. "Two Type D sightings at twenty thirty-two and twenty-three hundred hours precisely," reported the skinny man.

"What's a Type D sighting?" I asked.

"Confirmed sighting of illuminated object in stratosphere, trajectory unknown," he replied.

Huh? Again Bushy Beard translated for us. "Light in the sky. Maybe a plane, maybe a helicopter…"

"Maybe something else…" added the woman with frizzy hair.

"And I'll bet we weren't the only ones who saw them," said the woman in glasses darkly.

"Great," I said with as much enthusiasm as I could muster. (Not much. I mean, they kept watch for hours and hours, and all they had seen was just one more aeroplane!)

Just then the door opened and Cathy led in a little old lady. "This is the breakfast room. You can sit right there, Mrs Appleby," said my sister. "Can I get you tea or coffee?"

The old woman nodded sweetly and shuffled to her chair in her pink, fluffy slippers. As she sat down she murmured

"Good afternoon," to everyone. I glanced at my watch – it was 8.30 in the morning. When did she arrive? I wondered. Whatever, this meant the B&B was completely full now, and that had to be a good thing.

I walked round the table and smiled at the old lady.

"Good morning," I said. "How would you like your egg done?"

The old woman smiled and bobbed her head at me. She was wearing a big baggy cardigan. The sleeves were so long that they completely covered her hands. "Egg," she said. Perhaps she hadn't heard me.

"Your egg," I repeated. "Would you like it fried, boiled or scrambled?"

"Oh, yes," said Mrs Appleby. "Fried, boiled or scrambled." Then she added, "Hello. Thank you."

Great, I thought as I went back to the kitchen. We've got the B&B full, but it's full of five UFO-nuts, and one little old lady who doesn't seem to know where she is. I remembered a saying I had once heard: be careful what you wish for ... it might come true.

Chapter 7

Later that morning, Eddie and I were sitting around. I wanted to be in the house to see what the STUFFO people did next. Eddie just wanted to sit around.

We sat and waited. Mum had gone out to the shop. No sign of STUFFO yet – they were probably catching up on their sleep.

I jumped up when I heard a noise from the hall. It was only my sister, putting her coat on, but there was something odd about her expression.

"What's the matter?" I asked. "You look like you've seen a spider in the bathtub." Cathy shook her head. "A lizard under your bed? A goldfish in the sink?"

Cathy was about to answer when Mrs Appleby started down the stairs. The old woman still had her slippers on and the buttons on her cardigan were all done up wrong.

"I'm going for a walk with Mrs Appleby," said Cathy. "We won't be long."

"Less than one hour," beamed the old woman, "which is fifty … no, tell a lie, sixty minutes."

My polite smiled reappeared.

"Now then, dear," said Mrs Appleby to Cathy as they left the house, "tell me more about all the pretty flowers you have round here."

I wandered back to the living room, but I didn't get much peace that morning. I had hardly sat down when the doorbell rang. It was someone looking for a room for the night. Ten minutes later someone else came round, and not long after that someone telephoned for a room. And it didn't stop there. In the next hour I had to answer the door two more times and the phone three more times. And each time I had to give the same two answers: "Sorry, we're all booked up," and "No, I haven't seen any aliens." I was starting to feel like a parrot, saying the same phrases over and over.

When the doorbell rang yet again, I groaned, "Must be yet another person after a room." But the woman at the door this time didn't look like the other UFO spotters. Also her trendy clothes and wide-brimmed, floppy hat were sure signs that she wasn't from round here (where green wellies are still considered daring fashion statements). She was talking into a mobile phone. When she saw me she said, "... must run, daahling. Work calls!"

"Hello, can I help?" I asked.

"Ye-es, I'd like to speak to the owner," said the woman in a posh voice. She looked over the top of my head into the hall behind me, expecting to see a grown-up.

"My mum's out," I answered. "But if you're looking for a room, we're all booked up."

The woman gave a weak smile at the idea of her staying in our B&B.

"No, no, no – I'm after information, that's all. My name is Sarah Blethington-Watkins. I work for Midland Television."

"Really?" said an eager voice from behind me. Might have known Eddie wouldn't want to miss out.

"Yes, I'm a researcher on *Dirk Glib's World of the Unknown*. You're familiar with it, no doubt..."

Of course! It was that stupid show Cathy watched – Dirk Glib with his plastic, perfect hair and his dazzlingly white teeth, travelling round the country investigating the world of ghosts and mind-reading and abominable snowmen ... and UFO sightings! A warning bell went off in my brain.

"Dirk Glib isn't coming here, is he?" I asked.

"Well, that remains to be seen," said Sarah Blethington-Watkins. "It all depends on what I discover. If I find enough material for a programme, then Dirk might come up here to do a show."

"And what have you found so far?"

The woman sniffed. "Not much. The usual old stuff about a mysterious light in the sky." She let out a heavy sigh. "It's always the same. Everyone gets into a flap, and what they've seen always turns out to be an aircraft or a weather balloon or a shooting star or a satellite. Sometimes even a kite! I mean, can you imagine?" She leaned forward and her voice dropped a notch. "Before you know it, you'll be getting a visit from those anorak-wearing fanatics at STUFFO."

"They're here already," I said.

The researcher rolled her eyes. "Oh, I suppose they're harmless," she said. "And anyway, once they've been here a day or two and seen nothing, they'll toddle back to wherever they came from – they always do – and all this fuss will die down."

"You're not much of a believer in the world of the unknown, are you?" asked Eddie.

The young woman shook her head sadly. "I hate it, but this was the only job I could get in television," she said bitterly. "I wanted to work on the arts magazine programme, not trudge through the mud looking at stone monuments or giant footprints in the mountains ... not work for Dirk Glib who believes in all this nonsense and bosses us all around and – " She stopped herself. "Anyway, mustn't complain," she said (more to herself than to us). She pulled a card from her bag. "If anything else happens around here, be a darling and give us a call at the studio, would you?"

I turned the card over in my hand – it had her name and telephone number on it, and a picture of Dirk Glib trying to look all moody.

Then Sarah Blethington-Watkins whirled around back towards her car. As she went, she punched the buttons on her mobile phone again. "No luck, I'm afraid," I heard her say. "I don't think there's much of a story here. Another false alarm, I fear."

I turned to face Eddie.

"Close call, eh? Dirk Glib is the last person we want round here."

But Eddie had that thoughtful look on his face again. A single thought popped into my brain:

Chapter 8

Here's how Eddie explained it to me – he said that Sarah Blethington-Watkins was right. If we didn't do anything else, then the whole story would just die off in a few days. The villagers would start convincing themselves that their eyes had been playing tricks on them. The members of Stuffo would get fed up, zip up their anoraks and drive off in their battered van. And then we would be left alone with our view of the chemical factory and no guests staying at the B&B. Back to square one, in other words.

"So what can we do?" I asked glumly.

Eddie was as enthusiastic as I was glum. "One more thing," he said. "Just to make sure..."

So that's how we ended up sitting on the Number 23 into town that afternoon. We hadn't gone far when we spotted Cathy outside. She was still out for a walk with Mrs Appleby.

The two were deep in conversation and the old woman was clutching a large bunch of plants and flowers that she had picked.

They spotted us too. Mrs Appleby raised both hands in a wave and she shouted to us. It was hard to hear her over the noise of the bus, but it sounded like "Good night, girls!"

As the bus rumbled its way along the country lanes, I found myself staring out of the window at the overcast skies.

"Eddie, tell me something, will you? Why do you think people are so keen to believe that aliens are visiting us here?"

Eddie was only half-listening. He was too busy counting up all the spare change from his pockets. "Dunno," he said. "Those STUFFO people are a bit crazy, aren't they?"

I shook my head. "Yeah, but that doesn't explain the people in the village, does it? It's like you said – everyone wants to believe it. What I don't get is why..."

"Maybe it's just a nice break from the usual routine." Eddie shrugged. "Why do you think?"

"I don't know. I mean, there are so many stars out there, it stands to reason there's life on some of them. But why should they want to check us out?" It was hard putting it into words, but I did my best. "I think it's that people don't want to think we're all alone here."

"What, on this bus?"

"On this planet. I mean, it's nice to think there's some friendly alien checking up on us every so often, just to see if we're OK. You know what I mean?"

There was something about this thought that made me oddly sad, though I wasn't sure why. It didn't matter because Eddie hadn't even heard me. "Yeah, right," he said, and he showed me the pile of cash he had in his cupped hands. "That should be enough!" he grinned. "Time to go shopping!"

36

Chapter 9

After dinner that evening Eddie sneaked down to the garden shed, where we had hidden all the stuff we bought. I told him I would be there in a few minutes and I dashed to my room to dig out my old flippers. They had lain unused at the bottom of my wardrobe ever since I persuaded Mum to buy them for me at a car-boot sale.

On the landing I ran into Cathy. She had an even more distracted look on her face than usual – as if she had so many big ideas whirling around her mind that she had no time for the details of everyday life around her. (I hate it when she acts like that.)

"Hey, I need to tell you something," I said. "It's important." I wanted to explain to her what Eddie and I were about to do – why we thought it had to be done for the sake of the B&B. Really, I wanted her to say it was OK, I suppose.

But Cathy didn't stop. "Whatever it is, it'll have to wait," she said firmly, and she marched off towards the room where the old lady, Mrs Appleby, was staying. I had no idea what she was up to, and no time to find out.

I crept out to the garden shed where Eddie was still getting himself ready. Half an hour later we were all done. So that's how we ended up putting on our stupid alien-outfits and waddling up towards the house. And that's where you came in, remember?

When we got to the vegetable patch, Eddie whispered, "This is far enough. Let's get started."

As we had discussed, we both began picking up bits of plant and vegetables. We stuffed them into a sports bag, which no longer looked like a sports bag because we had decorated it with silver foil as well. (Have you ever noticed how in films everything aliens have is so silver and shiny?)

"Hey," I whispered. "Don't pull so many carrots up. My mum'll go crazy!"

But Eddie was really acting the part now. He held up a carrot near his green face and tilted his head from side to side as if he was studying the vegetable for the first time.

That's when we heard a faint noise from the back of the house – click, click, click. It was the sound of several cameras taking photos – five cameras, to be exact.

That was our sign to get going. We didn't want to be still in the vegetable patch when one of STUFFO grew brave enough to attempt their "first meeting".

"Let's go!" I hissed.

And let me tell you – it's not easy running in flippers and all that other gear, but we did a pretty good job legging it out of there.

Chapter 10

The next day was when our troubles really began.

When I came downstairs, Eddie was nowhere to be seen. Cathy wasn't in the house either, but I could see her outside, through the back window. She was out in the garden with Mrs Appleby again, heading off on another of their nature walks.

Mum was talking angrily into the phone in the hallway. "For the last time," she was saying into the receiver, "I didn't see anything unusual last night!"

I slipped past her and into the breakfast room. Four of the five members of STUFFO were hunched around the table. I expected them to be happy and noisily excited – after all, last night they had at long last seen what they had been waiting years for – but instead they spoke in low whispers and exchanged serious glances as if they were planning a bank robbery. I saw that there were some photos spread out in front of them – it was hard to make them out from this distance, but I could see two odd-looking pale figures. So the pictures had been developed already!

When Bushy Beard saw that I was in the room, he coughed loudly and swept all the photos up. Then he turned and gave me a big artificial smile.

"Morning, lad. Can we help you?" he asked, as if there was nothing unusual going on. It was a pretty bad act, but I knew I had to play along with it. I searched my brain for something to say.

"Nice day," I offered.

"Despite the slight precipitation, the atmospheric conditions are satisfactory," answered the skinny man. I think it was his attempt at small talk.

"He means yes," said Bushy Beard, "but it's a pity it's drizzling."

Maybe not such a pity, I thought. The drizzle would cover up any flipper-footprints that might give Eddie and me away.

Suddenly the frizzy-haired woman burst into the room.

"Quick!" she cried in panic. "The story's on TV!"

There was a scraping of chair-legs and a thumping of anxious footsteps as all five of them dashed into the TV room. I followed.

The news reader on TV was saying:

... just two nights after police received reports of strange lights in the sky. I repeat, this story just in. Unconfirmed reports of a sighting of a non-terrestrial life form near the village of Craigarth last night. Our sources say that photographs of the aliens may have been taken.

I expected the members of STUFFO to let out a great cheer. But Bushy Beard just groaned and turned the volume down, cutting the news reader off. The room was silent except for the ticking of the clock. At last Bushy Beard said, "This is terrible." The others nodded in solemn agreement.

"But why?" I asked, puzzled. "I mean, you've got the photos, haven't you? You'll be famous. What's the problem?"

Their gaze fell on me. They no longer bothered trying to pretend that there were no photos.

"Your perception of the variables involved in this predicament is insufficient," said the skinny man.

"He means you don't understand," said Bushy Beard (He got no argument about this from me). "STUFFO is an organization dedicated to a friendly first encounter between humans and life from other planets. But not everyone thinks like us..." I didn't like the sound of this.

42

The woman in glasses spoke. She looked as though all her worst fears had come true. "It's what I've been saying for ages. Some people will just be interested in making money out of it. Like that Glib character on TV – sure, he talks about it, but he's not interested in a first meeting. He's just interested in TV ratings. If people like that ever did meet an alien, they'd want to stick it in a circus and make people pay to see it."

The man with the bowl-haircut whispered something to the frizzy-haired woman. "Or stick it on TV," she repeated glumly. "Worse still, others will think that just by visiting our planet, aliens must want to take it over. And if they think it's an invasion, then they'll want to strike back."

"It could be a disaster," said Bushy Beard glumly. "But what I don't understand is this: how was the story leaked? We were the only ones who saw the visitors ... weren't we? Who could have called the press?"

But I knew exactly who. Eddie! I spun round and dashed out of the room. In the hallway Mum had just put down the phone yet again.

"Hey, what's going on round here? I want to ask you a thing or two, my lad," she shouted, but I didn't stop. I raced out of the back door and up the garden.

Chapter 11

As I charged through the gate, I noticed several cars parked in the lane. When they spotted me, five or six people leapt out and ran up to me. A scruffy-looking man with a pencil and notebook demanded, "Can you answer a few questions, sonny?" At the same time a woman thrust a microphone in my face: "Just tell us what you saw, in your own words."

Reporters! They swarmed around me, jostling and shoving each other for position. This was becoming terrible – it felt as if I was sinking deeper and deeper into a quicksand of trouble. I was already up to my neck and I didn't want to sink any further. I certainly didn't want to talk to any reporters. I shook my head and ran on, ignoring their shouts to stop.

But things were even worse in the village. A huddle of villagers looked on as the members of a television crew bustled around, unloading equipment from the back of a van and setting it up.

There was only one person not busy, and he was instantly recognizable. It was Dirk Glib, presenter of Dirk Glib's World of the Unknown. So he had decided to come and investigate the story, had he? He was holding his head to one side while an assistant dabbed make-up on his cheek.

Suddenly Glib jerked upright and waved the assistant away. He raised one hand to silence those around him, and he sniffed the air like a bloodhound making out the faintest scent on the breeze. His giant moustache twitched.

"I'm getting an odd feeling about this place," he announced. If things hadn't been so serious, I would have added that this place had an odd feeling about him. (At least, *I* did.)

The TV presenter squared his jaw. "Something strange is going on here – something really big – and Dirk Glib is the man to find out what." I thought it was an awful, pompous speech, but a small ripple of applause broke out from the crowd of villagers. Their faces still shone with excitement at all the new developments taking place in the village. I noticed also several fresh faces in the crowd – no doubt more UFO spotters who had made the trek to our village.

Glib ignored them all. "Sarah!" he snapped. "Where's that report on the sightings? Do I have to wait all day?"

A woman scurried forward with a clipboard and a stack of papers in her hands. It was Sarah Blethington-Watkins, the researcher who had visited the B&B. She looked unhappy and flustered now, as she began to read out the information to Glib. The presenter listened, tapping his foot impatiently.

I edged forward to see if I could hear more, but Glib fixed me with a glare as cold as a polar bear's underpants.

"What do you want, kid?" he snarled. "No autographs today, so clear off! You can watch me on TV, same as everyone else." Then he turned away and barked more orders at the crew around him. Sarah Blethington-Watkins gave me a weak smile as if to say sorry for her boss, but I had more important things on my mind. I turned on my heels and ran.

I had no way of knowing for sure where Eddie had gone, but somehow I guessed where he would be. I raced out of the village and ran towards Celts Hill, and then all the way up the footpath that snaked its way to the top. Sure enough, Eddie was up there, calmly chewing on a blade of grass.

He squinted up at me. "So how is Phase 2 going?" he asked.

"Terrible!" I gasped. "There's reporters all outside our house and the story even made it on to TV!"

Eddie seemed satisfied. "Well, great! I called them pretty early, but I didn't expect it to make the news until they got hold of the photos. Anyway, this should be enough coverage, I reckon. No problems with the old B&B now." He stretched his arms in a lazy yawn.

"No!" I cried. "It's getting too serious! There's going to be reporters and camera crews and UFO spotters everywhere! We're going to get found out!"

"Relax," smiled Eddie, and I noticed he still had a bit of green face-paint behind one of his ears. "I mean, it's a good laugh, isn't it?"

I couldn't believe it. But then I looked down at that big grin still on Eddie's face and suddenly I realized that that's what all this was to him – "a good laugh". He may have wanted to help the B&B out, but that was not his main reason for carrying on with the hoax. He was enjoying it. I felt a sudden stab of anger towards my old friend.

"Are you crazy? We're going to be in big trouble. We're going to –"

I stopped abruptly. "Hold on a minute," I said. "Did you see that? That bush down there just moved!"

Eddie sat up and followed my finger to a bush down below us. It swayed in the breeze a little. Then it scurried several feet forward.

"What the – " I felt as if the whole world had just decided to go crazy.

The bush continued to move steadily onwards. It was joined by several bushes around it. They all began moving up the hill.

Walking bushes? What next? Would the sun pop out from behind a cloud and wink at us? Would the trees in the distance start to do the twist?

I could tell that Eddie was just as amazed as I was. His mouth hung open but no words came out (and, trust me, things have to be pretty amazing to stun Eddie into silence).

As I watched the formation of bushes scuttle forward, an awful idea crept into my mind. Maybe it was true, maybe these were –

Before I could finish that thought, we were surrounded by a squad of soldiers. They all wore camouflage gear and had bits of twigs and shrubbery poking out of their helmets. The moving bushes were soldiers – soldiers who were now glaring at us as though we might be the enemy.

"Stay right where you are, lads!" ordered a stocky corporal. That wasn't difficult – I was too scared to move anyway.

One of the other soldiers stepped forward. He was holding some kind of machine, which had a red flashing light

on it. He held it first over me, and then Eddie. All the while the machine let out a steady beeping noise as regular as the ticking of a clock.

"They're all clear," said the soldier.

"Clear of what?" I asked.

"Never you mind, sonny boy," said the corporal. "This is a matter of national security. You two lads just run along home, eh?"

And then the whole squad of bushes began moving off down the other side of the hill, leaving us gulping in amazement.

When the soldiers were out of earshot, I scrambled to my feet and glared at Eddie. "You can do what you want," I said, "but this has gone too far for me. It's got out of hand. I'm going to tell the truth."

Chapter 12

I was out of breath by the time I had legged it all the way home. Then I had to battle my way through the line of reporters. Finally, I made it back into the house. No one around. In the kitchen there was a note on the table from my mum.

Someone from the army came round.
I have gone to answer a few questions. Unless it's an absolute emergency, I want you to stay in the house.

So, the army had been here too. I was pretty sure that they would not stop at interviewing just one person from the house. They would want to talk to everyone, and when they got to me... I knew that I would rather get it all over with and confess that it was all a hoax and we were responsible for it. I started rooting in the drawer for the key to the garden shed. That was where we had hidden our alien gear.

Suddenly I became aware that I was being watched. I whirled around. Cathy, my little sister, was standing in the doorway observing me. I realized with a start that I hadn't even spoken to her for a day. Now that I was going to confess everything, she would be a good person to start with.

"Cathy," I said, "you were right. I want to tell you that –"

She held up one hand as if to say "Enough". There was a funny look on her face – serious and somehow awe-struck at the same time. "Before you say anything else," she said, "there's someone I want you to talk to. It's Mrs Appleby…"

What? I knew that Cathy had been spending a lot of time with our visitor, but why did she want me to speak to her?

"But –"

Again Cathy cut me off. "No questions, Tom," she said, taking me by the arm. "It'll all make sense in a few minutes."

When we got upstairs she rapped gently on the door to Mrs Appleby's room. A voice called out for us to come in.

When we stepped inside, the old lady was sitting in an easy chair. She was wearing the same baggy cardigan which looked about four sizes too big. She gave Cathy a friendly nod, then squinted as she looked me up and down.

"Evening, Tom," said Mrs Appleby, apparently unaware that it was late morning. The big comfy chair made her look small and frail. She smiled and clicked off the TV with the remote control.

"Good show, that," she said. "Very amusing." She had been watching the news.

Cathy stepped further into the room, leading me in too. "Ask Mrs Appleby how she got here," my sister said to me. There was something odd about her voice.

I sighed, thinking, "What is this all about?" As if I didn't have enough on my mind! We had more reporters outside our door than the Royal Family did. The army had set up camp in the area. There were probably UFO spotters all over the place, with more on the way – not to mention Dirk Glib and his TV cameras. But still my sister wanted me to have a polite chat with this little old lady?

"OK... how did you get here, Mrs Appleby?"

"Up the stairs, same as you, dear," said the old lady.

"Oh." I turned to go, but Cathy gripped my arm. "No, ask Mrs Appleby how she got here to the village."

I asked the question.

The old lady smiled sweetly and blinked behind the thick lenses of her glasses. "I came in my spaceship," she said. "My friends were kind enough to drop me off. They'll be back for me in about ten of your whatsits ..." She searched for the word. "... *hours.*"

Now what could I say to that? Great, I thought, just what I needed! Our other guest was even barmier than STUFFO. She didn't just believe in UFOs, she thought she had arrived in one!

But all I said – as politely as I could – was, "How nice for you."

"I think you'd better show him," said Cathy quietly.

And then it happened. The little old lady put down her knitting. Then she reached up to her hairline and ... get ready for this ... she pulled her face right off. Honest! She pulled her face off as if it was a mask and underneath was the most alien face you could imagine. It was sort of insect-like, but a bit like a crab's face as well. Then again, it was kind of lizardy, with a bit of fish thrown in. It was ... oh, listen, it was WEIRD. Just look at the picture and you'll see what I mean.

When I finally pulled my eyes away from that face, I realized that the Mrs Appleby-thing no longer had arms – at least not human arms. Now she had these long, pink tentacles that waved and wiggled out of the sleeves of her oversized, woolly cardigan.

I was frozen to the spot, too terrified and stunned to move a muscle. But my heart was beating as wildly as a heavy metal drum solo. And then the creature spoke. Its mouth widened and I saw a line of drool run between two sets of mean-looking choppers. Its voice was a kind of high-pitched buzzing, and what it said was:

"By gum, that's better. That face was starting to itch like crazy."

And that's when I fainted.

Chapter 13

I woke up slowly, drifting to the surface like a diver rising from the depths of the ocean. I had a strange feeling that I was leaving behind a weird nightmare, though I couldn't remember what.

Then I opened my eyes. Cathy was kneeling in front of me, and behind her Mrs Appleby – the human-looking Mrs Appleby, that is – was leaning forward worriedly.

"Are you quite all right, dear?" said the old woman. The expression on her face was concerned, but I knew what lay underneath that face. I began to scramble backwards in fear.

"Oh, don't be so childish!" snapped Cathy impatiently. (I hate it when she says that.) "What sort of way is that to treat a guest to this planet? Mrs Appleby might be an alien, but she's not going to zap you or fry your brain or anything. Are you, Mrs Appleby?"

The old woman blinked. "Not unless I'm supposed to, dear. I don't want to seem rude."

I sat up and tried to will my brain to comprehend it all. "Wha– what's going on?" I asked at last. This seemed to be my catch-phrase lately.

"I do think he needs an explanation," agreed Cathy. She seemed remarkably calm under the circumstances. (That's my sister for you.) The thing known as Mrs Appleby nodded.

"Well," said the old woman, "it's like this. My people live on a planet far from your solar system." I still couldn't quite believe this – here was this little old lady in a cardigan, talking like a bad science-fiction show on TV. "We are well aware of your planet, though we have a policy of letting you develop on your own. We keep an eye on you, though, by monitoring your television and radio broadcasts."

The old lady leaned forward and winked. "To be honest, we quite enjoy a lot of it – especially soap operas ... very amusing, those."

I tried to picture it. It was hard to imagine a bunch of weird-looking, multi-tentacled aliens sitting around watching *EastEnders* and *Neighbours*. Did they think such programmes were a slice of real life on another planet? When they went out, did they use some advanced alien technology to tape the episodes they were missing? These questions and many more whirled around inside my head, but I only asked the most obvious one: "What are you doing here?"

Mrs Appleby's smile broadened. "Well, we were in the neighbourhood – your solar system, that is – when we caught the news about the UFO sighting. We knew it wasn't us, so we were intrigued. I decided to come for a closer look."

"You mean you're not here to ...?" I let the question trail off, but Mrs Appleby knew what I meant.

"Consider me a tourist. I'm just here for a visit, and I must say I've had a jolly time so far, thanks to you. Very entertaining, it's all been," she smiled. "I introduced myself to your sister, but you were so busy that I didn't really want to bother you."

A thought popped into my head. "So what are you really called? I mean, 'Mrs Appleby' doesn't sound very alien. Shouldn't you be called 'Zorg' or something like that?"

The alien old lady chuckled. "You're right, Mrs Appleby isn't my real name. My real name is Mrs Rogers."

My eyes opened wide in surprise, but Cathy just snorted with laughter and hit the old lady playfully on the arm. "Tell the truth!" It seemed that even aliens made bad jokes.

Mrs Appleby smiled. "My real name is…" And then the old-lady-that-wasn't-really-an-old-lady let out a sound that was a cross between a hippo's bellow and a jet taking off. I couldn't even begin to spell it for you (and I'm a good speller).

I attempted to smile back. "It suits you," I said.

"My friends are finishing up a science expedition on the planet you call Neptune," said Mrs Appleby. "They'll pick me up this evening at …" She looked at her cheap plastic wristwatch. "… sixty to eleven, on the dot. Up on top of that big hill."

Cathy began to explain the complexities of telling the time earth-style. It was easy to imagine a newcomer finding it a bit confusing: sixty seconds in a minute and sixty minutes in an hour, but just twenty-four hours in a day. Why not just do it all in multiples of 10? At last, we established that the time she had meant was ten o'clock.

But a sudden feeling of panic gripped me. "Hold on. You don't want anyone else to find out you're here, do you?"

Both my sister and the visitor shook their heads. "Oh no, I've got strict instructions not to make any … official contact," said Mrs Appleby. "There'd be a terrible fuss."

"Well, you may have to change your plans," I said. "You see, there are reporters all over the place…"

Cathy smiled patiently. "It's OK. We'll just do what you and Eddie wanted me to do in the first place – say nothing. Just sit tight for the afternoon. It'll be getting dark by ten. We can sneak Mrs Appleby out of the house and send her safely on her way."

But the words began to tumble out of me. "No, you don't understand. That Dirk Glib is here too. He's a creep, but it's as if he can sense that something weird is going on. And that's not all … the army's here! We ran into a squad of soldiers and they had some kind of machine with them. I think they were using it to search for …" I glanced at Mrs Appleby, "… for alien life-forms. They're searching the whole area, they're bound to come here sooner or later. And if they find you …"

My unfinished sentence seemed to hang in the air like a storm cloud on the horizon. The smile had vanished from Cathy's face.

"At the very least they'll take Mrs Appleby away for questioning. The soldier we talked to said it was a matter of national security."

Cathy began to chew her thumbnail anxiously. Mrs Appleby didn't seem too concerned. "Oh no, dear, I'm afraid I can't do that. You see, we can only survive for so long away from our home planet and we've been travelling for some time now. As soon as my friends pick me up, we've got to go straight home." The way she said it, it sounded as though she would be taking a bus trip to a bingo hall, not travelling light years across the universe.

"Is there any way you can get in touch with your friends?" asked my sister. "Get them to pick you up early?"

"I'm afraid not, dear," said Mrs Appleby, still not understanding the danger she could be in. But Cathy and I swapped nervous glances.

"What are we going to do?" I whispered.

Neither of us knew the answer to that question and we were silent for several long moments. But then, as if in reply, a door slammed and a voice boomed out from downstairs. It was Eddie, and his voice sounded somehow different – urgent and serious, for once.

"Tom!" he shouted. "Come quickly! There's going to be a press conference in the village!"

I looked quickly at my sister and Mrs Appleby. "You stay here. I'll go and find out what I can."

"Very nice, dear," said the alien life form, picking up her knitting.

Eddie was waiting for me at the bottom of the stairs. He looked at me guiltily. "I've been thinking," he said. "You were right – I was treating it all like a big joke. But not any more – there are some army bigwigs in the village. Everyone's expecting them to announce something big at this press conference. It IS all getting too serious."

If only you knew HOW serious, I thought. But there would be plenty of time for that. I remembered Mum's note telling us not to leave the house. Unless it was an emergency! You couldn't get much more of an emergency than this, could you? I mean, it was a matter of life and death, wasn't it?

"Let's go, then," I said.

Chapter 14

The village was packed with people – villagers, soldiers, UFO spotters, reporters armed with cameras, Dirk Glib's TV crew. A podium had been set up right outside the village shop. There was a feeling of nervous anticipation as the crowd waited for the conference to begin. Eddie and I wormed our way through the mass of people until we got to a place where we could see everything that was going on.

The crowd quietened down when an army officer strode up to a row of microphones that had been set up. He cleared his throat and began to read from the piece of paper he held.

"We have called this press conference to put an end to the speculation," he began. "The army was called here after a number of reports of … unusual sightings. Since we arrived, we have employed an experimental new machine." (I knew he was talking about the machine Eddie and I had seen.) "And we can now confirm that we have recorded some unusual readings which indicate the presence of … extraterrestrial activity in the area."

A strange hush fell over the crowd. Of course, this is what they had expected to hear – that it was true, that aliens had visited the village. But somehow it was still shocking to hear it said by someone who looked so official. But there was something else that shocked the crowd: this officer wasn't just saying that aliens *had* visited...

A single voice spoke up and asked the question that was on everyone's mind. It was Dirk Glib. I would know that arrogant tone anywhere. The TV presenter fixed the officer with a stare as unblinking as that of an owl in a staring contest.

"Are you saying that there might still be aliens in the area?" he said.

The officer rubbed his chin thoughtfully. "Please don't jump to conclusions. As I said, there is some evidence that ..." But the crowd broke out in an uproar, cutting him off. Dozens of camera flashed as the reporters took photos of the historic moment.

When the hubbub died down, it was Glib who spoke again.

Where are they then? The aliens?

The officer took off his beret and scratched the stubble on top of his head. "We're not exactly sure. The technology we are using is still very new. Our scientists are making final adjustments to it, and we expect all the problems to be ironed out in the next few hours. We have a team working on it right now. And then, ladies and gentlemen … if any alien is still in the area, we will find it."

The conference went on – something about the village being a military zone now, and the activity of the press being controlled by the army – but I only half-listened.

Eddie looked at me with big eyes. "What's going on, Tom?" he asked quietly.

I returned my friend's anxious stare. "Eddie, if you've got any more of your brilliant plans," I said, "now's the time to come up with one. Let's head back to the B&B. There's something I want to show you."

Chapter 15

Later that afternoon seven of us sat at the breakfast room table. I looked around at the five members of STUFFO, and a pale-looking Eddie. Three guesses why he was looking pale? That's right – Eddie had had a Type A close encounter with Mrs Appleby.

But there was also a new determination in my friend. He rose and gave us all a serious look. "I suppose you're wondering why we asked you here," he said to the five UFO spotters. (I think he'd heard someone in a film say that once.)

"Affirmative," said the skinny man.

"Yes," agreed the others. The woman in glasses looked around the room suspiciously. I think she was looking for hidden microphones or something.

Eddie took a deep breath and told them everything. I won't repeat what he said, because it's all stuff that you know already. But, as you'd probably expect, it was an emotional afternoon for the members of STUFFO. At first they were furious (when they heard about the hoax). Then Cathy brought in Mrs Appleby. For a long time they all just sat in stunned disbelief. After spending all of their time waiting for this moment – a genuine, Type A meeting with an alien – they were so shocked they didn't even know what to say. The silence stretched out, then at last one of the members of STUFFO spoke. It was the man with the bowl-haircut and, for the first time ever, I could hear him loud and clear.

"Hello," he said, with a shy smile.

That broke the silence and we got on with the meeting. When we explained the problem, they shared our sense of anxiety about getting Mrs Appleby safely home.

"But what can we do?" asked Bushy Beard. "The army's already here. It's too late, isn't it? It's only a matter of time before they find her."

It felt now like we were in some top-secret meeting. It seemed that there should be important documents on the table in front of us, rather than a sugar bowl and a variety pack of breakfast cereals.

Eddie gave us all a steely smile. "Don't worry," he said. "I have a plan."

"That's nice," said the alien in the pink slippers.

Chapter 16

If you had been watching TV that evening, this is what you would have seen.

Half-way through a game show the screen goes blank and the announcer says, "We interrupt this programme to bring you a news flash. We go now to Dirk Glib, live from the village of Craigarth."

Ladies and gentlemen, the army has cleared the streets of Craigarth. But that will not stop Dirk Glib, for one of the most important events in human history is about to take place – a meeting between humanity and an alien life form.

Dirk Glib appears on the screen. The village lies behind him in darkness. He gives the camera his most sincere look and holds the mike to his chin.

He pauses to let the news sink in, then says,

A few minutes ago I – Dirk Glib, investigative reporter – received information that these ... visitors from another world will appear here, any minute now.

You can almost feel the excitement from Glib. He senses that he is about to become the most famous reporter in the world. He looks as pleased with himself as a cat that not only has the cream, but is the owner of an entire dairy farm.

Several tense minutes pass, and then the camera picks up two strange figures in the background. They waddle slowly towards the camera bobbing their hairless green heads. Their big flat feet slap on the ground.

Glib's eyes are huge. When the two are close enough he lifts one hand.

Greetings, I am Dirk Glib. As representative of the people of Earth, I am proud to welcome you to our planet.

The two strange figures, who are standing by the duck pond, fix him with silver eyes. They put their heads together as if trying to figure out what he has said.

Suddenly there is the roar of engines and the squeal of brakes as several jeeps and army trucks pull up. Dozens of soldiers clamber out and point their rifles at the two figures.

"Wait!" cries Glib, before the troops advance. "What message do you have for us?"

The tension is awful. Everyone is waiting for the answer. Do they come in peace? Is this the beginning of a terrible invasion? Then one of the two strange figures steps slowly forward and its face breaks out into a great big grin.

"I have only one thing to say," says my friend, Eddie (for, of course, that's who it is).

He looks straight at the camera.

Chapter 17

"You two are in Big Trouble," said a soldier to us. He tried to sound gruff, but he finished it off with a cheerful wink for good measure.

It was nice of him to tell us, but we already knew. We were surrounded by soldiers. Others were questioning Dirk Glib and his crew. Glib's mouth was opening and closing in horror and shock. He looked like a goldfish in a bad mood. I pulled the swimming cap off and scratched my head. I flicked a glance at my watch. It was quarter to ten. Fifteen minutes until Mrs Appleby left. I just hoped that was enough time. We hadn't expected the army to arrive quite so quickly.

I felt spots of rain on my face. The green paint began to trickle and run down my cheeks. I was glad to get rid of it.

Just then someone else marched up to us. It was the officer who had given the press conference. He glared at us angrily. "Well, well, well … what are we going to do with you two?"

It was one of those questions that you're not really supposed to answer, so we just stood there with our heads hung low. I didn't mind about being told off. I knew that every moment they were spending dealing with us gave Mrs Appleby a better chance of getting away. That had been Eddie's plan – we were just the diversion, while the others helped her escape.

But before the officer could say anything else, a young soldier wearing earphones and carrying a radio ran up to him. "Sir!" he gasped. "Our scientists say they've sorted out the equipment. They've got a lock on the alien life form. It was in the house, the B&B! But it's not there now. It's moving towards Celts Hill."

"Quick!" ordered the officer. "Let's go!" There was a mad rush as all the soldiers piled back into their jeeps and trucks. Eddie and I were forgotten instantly. We just stood there in the middle of all the confusion, feeling the rain come down harder now.

The air was filled with the sound of engines roaring into life. They all headed off towards the hill.

I looked again at my watch. The hands had crawled round to ten to ten!

"Did we give them enough time?" I asked Eddie.

"I hope so," he said, green paint streaming down his face.

Someone ran up to us – it was Sarah Blethington-Watkins, the TV researcher. I couldn't see Glib or the rest of his crew anywhere.

"It was you two, wasn't it?" said the researcher. "You called Dirk up and tipped him off about this little meeting?" I nodded.

A tiny smile flickered across her face. "Well, you'd best follow this through to the very end. Come on, my car's parked over there. No one'll notice if we follow."

Chapter 18

She was right – no one stopped us and we followed the convoy of army trucks all the way to the foot of Celts Hill. The road ran out there, and they had all parked, blocking the way completely. Sarah Blethington-Watkins pulled up too and we jumped out of her car into the rainy night.

"I don't know what's going on, but good luck!" called the researcher as Eddie and I ran off. Soldiers were running all over the place. The night echoed with the bark of orders and the footfalls of dozens of heavy boots.

I looked back to wave my thanks, and saw that a corporal had begun to question Sarah. Eddie and I slipped away. We made our way to the foot of the hill, where a large group of soldiers were surrounding a battered old van. No one dared to do anything until the commanding officer arrived. With him was a man holding one of those little beeping machines. He wasn't wearing a uniform, and I guessed he must be a scientist. With shaking arms he held the machine out towards the back of the van. The machine's steady beep sped up wildly.

"There's one in there. Or at least it's been in there!" he gasped.

"Corporal," said the officer to one of his men. "Open it up!"

The corporal reached out a trembling hand and took hold of the door handle. All around us dozens of fingers tightened on triggers. The only sound was the hiss of the rain. The back door of the van creaked open.

Inside sat the five members of STUFFO and my sister Cathy. They were drinking cocoa and watching a portable television. I caught a glimpse of the screen – it was the scene back at the village – and I knew they had been following everything on the live TV report. There was a sigh of relief from the troops around me. I joined in, but for different reasons. I was relieved because the plan had worked so far.

While we had been distracting the army and Glib, STUFFO had managed to drive Mrs Appleby to the hill where she would be picked up by her friends. I looked at my watch. Four minutes to ten!

"Evenin'," said Bushy Beard pleasantly. The soldiers ignored him. The scientist twiddled with some buttons on the little machine and said, "Hold on. I'm getting an even stronger reading coming from ... the top of the hill!"

"Quick!" shouted the officer, and there was the clomp of boots as the soldiers began to run up the hill. Eddie and I followed. Behind us I heard all of the members of STUFFO scrambling out of the van. No one wanted to miss this.

It was hard getting up the hill in all that mud. Eddie and

I had pulled our flippers off, but that meant we were running in our socks, which wasn't much easier. I slipped and fell forward. Eddie took my arm and helped me up. "Come on," he panted. "It's less than two minutes to ten. We've got to get to the top. Stop them ... somehow." I got to my feet and carried on running.

"Look!" shouted Eddie, pointing toward the top of the hill. Beyond all of the soldiers making their way up, I could see a single figure at the very top of the hill. It had to be Mrs Appleby! Though she was only a dark shape against the night-time sky, I would recognize that baggy cardigan anywhere. But the soldiers were almost at the top of the hill too.

I looked once again at my watch. It was ten o'clock exactly! Thunder rumbled in the distance and then ... nothing.

I'm not sure what I expected to happen: a giant flying saucer to appear or Mrs Appleby to vanish in a puff of smoke as she was beamed up to her ship. But nothing happened at all. The rain just went on falling, and the soldiers went on running up the hill. The first of them made it to the top, and I lost sight of Mrs Appleby as they gathered round her.

I stopped running. I was panting and I had a stitch in my side, but worse than that was the sorrow I felt. We had failed! It was clear that Eddie felt the same way. He looked at me glumly and rested a hand on my shoulder.

"Maybe it'll be OK," he said, though he didn't sound very confident. I sat down in the mud and felt the rain strike my face.

It wasn't long before the troops began to make their way back down the hill. Several trudged wearily past us, not even bothering to comment on the strange sight we must have made. They had seen too many strange things that day to pay Eddie and me much attention, however weird we still looked.

Then the main body of soldiers came down the path, and in the middle of them was a familiar figure in a baggy cardigan and pink slippers. She beamed at us when she saw us, not bothered in the least by the rain.

"Hello, lads," said my mother. "Nice night for a walk!"

Mum? It wasn't Mrs Appleby at all. It was my mum, but she was wearing Mrs Appleby's baggy old cardigan. She even had the fluffy pink slippers on too, though they were soaked and covered in mud (and so not very fluffy any more). I was too stunned to say anything. But Eddie's face lit up. "Not bad, Mrs Campbell," he called out, and he held up one of the flippers he had tucked under his arm. "But would you like to borrow one of these?"

Chapter 19

Thirty minutes later I was sitting inside a tent at the base the army had set up. They had driven us there immediately and then split us up. I guessed we were all being interviewed separately to see if our stories matched up.

The officer opposite watched me carefully. My mind raced. I knew I couldn't slip up here.

"So let me get this straight," said the officer. "You're saying the whole thing was a hoax?"

I nodded.

"Carried out by you and your friend?"

I nodded again. (I probably looked like one of those stupid nodding dog toys you see in the back of cars.)

The officer asked me question after question – often the same question, to see if I gave the same answer – but I stuck to my story. I told him about the balloon and the silly costumes, but I never mentioned Mrs Appleby.

The interview wasn't bad, really. They didn't shine a light in my eyes or shout or try to trick me or anything like that. The officer just went on asking questions and noting down my answers. A soldier stood guard at the rear of the tent.

A thought occurred to me. The army hadn't ever wanted to capture or kill any aliens. They just wanted to find out what was going on. They had a job to do (and, after all, we'd certainly be glad of them if an unfriendly alien *did* decide to visit us here on the third planet from the sun). They weren't to know that Mrs Appleby wouldn't have survived if they'd detained her for even an hour or two.

After a while, another soldier burst in and told the officer that the other interviews were finished.

"Well," said the officer to me, "I suppose you're free to

go." Then he put his clipboard down and leaned closer.

"But just between you and me," he whispered, "I don't know what exactly went on here, but I know one thing ... I wish I'd seen it."

And that's when I realized – he was just as awe-struck as I was. The STUFFO woman with glasses, who thought that the government and the army knew all about UFOs, was wrong. There was no cover-up. I felt sorry that I couldn't tell this officer the whole truth, but I remembered that Mrs Appleby had said that it wasn't the right time yet for – what was the phrase she'd used? – "official contact".

And then they just let us go.

As we all trundled home in the battered van, Cathy told me everything that had happened.

"While you and Eddie were getting ready, Mum came home and found us all."

"I knew they were up to something," said Mum, folding her arms. "I'm not daft, you know." (I knew.)

"Anyway," continued Cathy, "we had to tell her everything. She didn't believe us at first, but then we introduced her to Mrs Appleby ... if you know what I mean."

"What did you think?" I asked Mum.

She shrugged. "I saw more shocking things when I was a nurse."

Cathy explained the rest. While Eddie and I did our thing in the village, they had all gone ahead with the plan, driving Mrs Appleby out to the hill, and Mum had gone along too. In the back of the van on the way she had had the idea that she should put on Mrs Appleby's cardigan and slippers – "just in case anything goes wrong," she said.

When they arrived there they had clambered up the hill, only to find Mrs Appleby's friends waiting. Cathy told me one of them had grumbled, "You're late," and the other had complained, "It's wet and cold here." Apparently they had been there on top of the hill waiting for an hour. Once again Mrs Appleby had failed to get the hang of telling Earth time.

Right before they had beamed up – there was no ship in sight, Cathy said – Mrs Appleby had turned to her and thanked her for a lovely visit. Then she had dug into her pocket and handed my sister a gift.

"What was it?" I asked, thinking it would be some incredible piece of super-advanced alien technology.

Cathy grinned and held out a white paper bag. "Boiled sweets. Would you like one?"

"Wonder where she is now?" said Eddie. It was the first time he'd spoken since we left the army base, and his voice was quiet and thoughtful.

"Going home," said my mum, and we all nodded and listened all the way back to the comforting pitter-patter of rain on the rooftop.

Chapter 20

Sarah Blethington-Watkins was right about one thing – the whole thing did die down after a while.

The army didn't stick around for long. Nor did the five members of STUFFO. Before they left, Bushy Beard slapped us all on the back and said we could be honorary members of STUFFO. The frizzy-haired woman hugged us all, and even the woman in glasses gave us a smile – I think she had decided at last that we weren't part of the government cover-up. The skinny man wished us "impending felicity" – I think he meant all the best for the future – and the man with the bowl-haircut mumbled something, but I couldn't hear what. The only word I had ever heard him utter was when he had seen Mrs Appleby in her true form.

As they all climbed back into their van to return to their jobs and daily lives, I realized that I would miss them. We had all been witnesses to an amazing event, and we knew that we would not be able to tell anyone else about it. Eddie, Cathy and I stood by the back gate and waved our goodbyes as the van coughed and hiccupped its way off down the road.

The reporters took a little longer to go, but at last they did. Our story was in all the newspapers for a while. Here were some of the headlines:

But then other stories hit the headlines:

The story of our hoax moved to the later pages and then out of sight all together.

The last thing I read about it was a tiny article in the local paper.

An army spokeswoman yesterday denied reports of faulty equipment in the Craigarth UFO investigation. She claimed that "the machine is very sensitive. The readings were probably affected because of the chemical factory nearby."

So the whole investigation was closed because of the factory! I had to chuckle when I read that.

Gradually everything went back to normal. Eddie didn't stay much longer either – his parents were pretty angry about what had happened – but before he left we found out what had happened to another person who had been involved in the whole affair. It was the middle of the day, but Eddie was watching TV. Suddenly he called me in from the other room. When I got there he was giggling and pointing at the screen.

It was a terrible programme for tiny kids. The presenters were a purple hand-puppet crocodile, called Egbert, and, dressed in a big jumper and trying as hard as he could to smile for the camera ... Dirk Glib! He looked about as happy as a bear that's just been told it's sprouts for dinner instead of honey.

I laughed out loud. "I heard his other show had been cancelled after what happened that night." (We had also received a jolly postcard from Sarah Blethington-Watkins, telling us the news. It also said that she had been given a job on a new arts programme.)

Eddie and I settled happily in front of the TV and chortled away as the hand-puppet crocodile squirted Glib right in the face with a water pistol.

"Everyone ought to do the job they're best suited to," grinned Eddie. "That's what I always say."

It was a perfect end to the weirdest summer ever.

Epilogue

But as it turned out, things weren't quite over yet.

We made it through the rest of the summer with the B&B doing OK. The village had received a lot of publicity with the story, so people were interested to come and stay and have a look around.

But the weather had turned lousy in the last week of the holidays. It was that time of year when you have to accept that, even if the sun puts in a brief encore appearance, the summer is pretty much over until next year.

So it was a bit of a shock when the doorbell rang. Mum wasn't in, and Cathy and I had a silent battle of wills about who would answer it. My nerve cracked first, so I went.

I opened the door and there, on our doorstep, was Mrs Appleby! And she wasn't alone, either. There were four other people with her. It was pretty clear that they too were not from round here – and I mean REALLY not from round here.

"Hello, dear," said Mrs Appleby, warmly. "I had such a nice time, I decided to come back for a proper holiday ... and bring my family too."

So that's how we started this new arrangement. Every year Mum is going to shut the B&B for a couple of months – at least, shut it to earthly visitors. That's the time when Mrs Appleby and her family stay with us. They're easy to look after too – you just have to plonk them in front of a telly and make sure they get plenty of salt in their cups of tea. They don't even get the beds messy, as they sleep propped up against the wall. (And if it goes well, they say they've got lots of friends who'd like to visit. So, one way or another, things are going to be fine with the B&B.)

So that's about all. As the great Dirk Glib once said, "It's a strange and mysterious world out there."

Hard to disagree when you've got a house full of aliens.